SE)

Surget, Alain

D1584073

First published in France by Éditions Flammarion MMVI

This edition published by Scribo MMX,
Scribo, a division of Book House, an imprint of
The Salariya Book Company
25 Marlborough Place, Brighton, BN1 1UB
www.book-house.co.uk
www.salariya.com
www.scribobooks.com

Copyright text and illustration © Éditions Flammarion MMVI

ISBN 978-1-907184-54-3

The right of Alain Surget to be identified as the author of this work and
the right of Annette Marnat to be identified as the illustrator of this work
has been asserted in accordance with sections 77 and 78 of the Copyright,
Designs and Patents Act, 1988.

English edition © The Salariya Book Company
& Bailey Publishing Associates MMX

Printed and bound in China

Translated by Jill Lewin

Editor: Shirley Willis

The text for this book is set in
1Stone Serif
The display types are set in
OldClaude

Written by
Alain Surget

Illustrated by
Annette Marnat

Translated by
Jill Lewin

THE PLUMED SERPENT'S GOLD

Ladies and gentlemen aboard!

The sunlight dancing on the sea made the waves shimmer like millions of pieces of gold stretching for as far as the eye could see. From his post at the top of the main mast, the lookout was finding it difficult to see, blinded as he was by the sparkling water. The Angry Flea had left Hispaniola and was sailing towards New Spain. Its captain, the Marquis Roger de Parabas, had found out that his fellow pirate, Captain Roc, was after a hoard of gold that the Spanish were planning to load onto ships there, in the port of Campeche. Parabas' plan was to find Captain Roc to offer him his children, Benjamin and Louise, in exchange for the map that revealed where his fabulous treasure was hidden.

Out on the ship's deck, Benjamin was painting the name El Cacahuete – meaning 'The Peanut' in Spanish – onto a wooden panel. His sister Louise was sitting on a coil of rope, desperately trying to thread the eye of a needle.

'I hope sea monsters eat these cursed pirates!' she hissed. 'I didn't escape from the orphanage in Paris just to find myself mending shirts and breeches for this motley crew. I've a good mind to leave this needle inside!'

'If you do that, you'll end up being thrown into the hold with your ankles in chains,' Benjamin warned her.

'I hope that rogue Parabas falls into father's hands. Then he'd rot in the hold like an old potato.'

'I wonder what happened to Red Mary,' Benjamin continued, arranging his paint and brushes.

'I hope she's gone to the devil!' snorted Louise, stabbing her needle hard into a piece of cloth.

'She is our half-sister, after all,' Benjamin protested.

'Ouch, I've pricked my finger! Let them all go to the devil!' cried Louise, tossing the breeches into the air. 'I'm fed up stitching my finger to their rags. Sick and tired of it!'

'Tirrred!' squawked the parrot, Shut-your-trap! from his perch in the rigging. 'Parrrabas will be angrrry! You'll be hung frrrom the main mast...'

'Oi, you – shut your trap!' Louise shouted, shaking her fist at him.

'Rrrououou!'

High up on the mast, the lookout had suddenly spotted something. Those shapes glinting on the water weren't just reflections but sails. And they were gaining on the Angry Flea!

'Three sails ahoy!' he yelled.

His cry set up a commotion on deck. Parabas ran to the prow and, putting his telescope to his eye, adjusted it to focus on the approaching ships.

'Raise the Spanish flag!' he ordered. 'And change the ship's name to El Cacahuete. Cover the figurehead with some cloth and you two men – pretend to be working on it.'

'Are these ships a danger to us?' asked On-the-Fence, the ship's first mate and second in command to Parabas.

'They're warships,' Parabas confirmed as the bosun shouted orders to the crew. 'They're stuffed to the main deck with cannons. We wouldn't stand a chance against them.'

'Shall I put the emergency plan into action?' On-the-Fence asked.

'Yes!' cried Parabas, focussing his telescope again. 'From now on, we're Spanish colonists sailing aboard El Cacahuete.'

Orders rang out from one end of the ship to the other. In an instant, the Spanish flag was flying high on the mast. Whilst one pirate nailed the panel with the newly painted El Cacahuete over the ship's real name at the stern, others rushed up from the hold clutching ladies and gentlemen's clothing.

'What's going on?' asked Louise in amazement. 'Are you going to put on a play?'

'In a way!' Parabas replied. 'It's all part of a pirate's kit, so that he can disguise himself as an old lady or a monk to fool the enemy. So put your needle down and put this dress on. You too,' he added, speaking to Benjamin.

'What?' retorted Benjamin. 'You want me to put on a frilly skirt and a hat? Don't even think about it! It's bad enough that my sister only wears men's clothing!'

'I haven't got time to argue,' growled the captain. 'Only those men with beards can wear hose, doublets and frock coats.'

The two children grudgingly obeyed, and soon a line-up of ladies, gentlemen and 'hidalgos' – Spanish noblemen – were leaning on the railing, watching the fleet of ships approach.

'Oi, you over there – put that pipe away!' hissed On-the-Fence. 'Have you ever seen a lady smoking a pipe? And hide your unruly hair under that bonnet!'

Those pirates who hadn't found costumes lay flat on the deck with arms at hand in case the Spanish saw through the deception. Only about five or six men dressed as sailors kept the ship on course. As for Parabas, he had swapped his green topcoat for a silk waistcoat and a muslin cravat.

One of the ships changed course slightly and as it came by to check out El Cacahuete, a mass of feathers dropped down beside the marquis.

'Open the gunporrrts, son of a sharrrk! Charrrge the cannons! Prrreparrre to be boarrrded!'

'Shut your trap, you pesky bird!' Parabas hissed, throwing his hat over the parrot.

'Stiflerrr! Barrrbarrrian! Ostrrrogoth! Rrrouououu!' came its muffled shrieks.

The Spanish ship was now less than ten metres away, her 24 cannons all at the ready in her gunports. Soldiers and officers stood in rigid lines, as stiff as waxworks.

'If one of them as much as sneezes, they'll all fall over,' Parabas chuckled to himself.

'Salute them!' he ordered under his breath. 'We'd better break the ice.'

On-the-Fence was the first to shout a greeting in Spanish. Then the pirates in disguise waved their arms, parasols and handkerchiefs and shouted 'yoo-hoo' in high-pitched voices.

'Where have you come from?' asked one of the Spanish officers.

'Florida,' Parabas replied. The Spanish captain made a gesture with his hand to signify 'good luck'.

'But... that girl is poking her tongue out at us,' one of his officers pointed out to him.

'Yes,' said the captain '...and she's still making faces at us now. Once we're a bit further away, fire a cannonball past their ears, just to teach her some manners.'

Parabas breathed a sigh of relief when the small fleet of ships was behind them.

'Keep in disguise,' he ordered the pirates. 'And you lot, don't stand up yet,' he added to the men stretched out on the deck. 'I'm sure they'll still be watching us through their telescopes.'

Louise went up onto the poop deck at the stern of the ship and started making even more faces and cheeky gestures.

'Can you see me okay?' she trilled. 'What about this? And that? And...'

There was a dull thud, then a whistling sound. The bosun grabbed Louise by the legs as the entire crew hit the decks. The cannonball passed under

the main sail, between the mast and the halyards, before shooting over the far side of the ship and landing in the water.

'They're attacking us!' yelled one of the men in a panicky voice.

'No, it's just a warning shot across our bows,' the bosun corrected him. 'Their way of paying this young lady back for pulling faces.'

Parabas leapt towards Louise, grabbed her by the arm and spun her round. He raised his hand, but Benjamin seized his arm.

'Don't you hit my sister!' he shouted. Parabas pushed him away. Hindered by the dress he was wearing, Benjamin fell over backwards. As fast as lightning, Louise seized the hilt of the sword Parabas wore at his side, pulled it out of its scabbard, sprang out of his grasp and pointed the blade at his chest.

'Now try and hit me!' she taunted him.

The bosun cocked his pistol and aimed it at Louise. Other pirates hitched up their skirts and rushed forward, armed to the teeth.

'Hide those weapons!' Parabas growled. 'Do you want the Spaniards to spot our ruse and return?'

Axes, pistols, rapiers and cutlasses all quickly disappeared again into the folds of their clothing.

'It's okay,' he went on, looking at Louise. 'I'll spare you the hiding you deserve for putting my ship in danger. Just give me my sword back.'

Louise stared at him, then she threw the weapon onto the deck and it rolled towards the helmsman's feet. The bosun picked it up and gave it to his captain.

'Shall I lock the little vixen up in the hold until we find Cap'n Roc?' he asked.

'Huh! There won't be enough room on the yards to hang all of you when my father finds out!' Louise retorted.

Parabas took his sword and walked away without saying a word.

'Why on earth did you do that?' Benjamin demanded. 'Pulling faces, I mean. Parabas was right! The Spaniards could have sunk the ship.'

'I didn't think they'd be so sensitive. I just

needed to have some fun, that's all. If you only knew how good it felt!'

The children leaned against the rail at the ship's stern, staring out to sea and letting their thoughts drift off with the silver wake left by the Angry Flea or, for the moment... El Cacahuete. Seated against the planking, One-Eyed Jack leant towards Scarface and muttered: 'Parabas must be mad giving those kids the run of the ship. Especially when we're so near the coast. Cap'n Roc's brats have brought us nothing but trouble instead of treasure. I dread what might happen next. I've a good mind to chuck 'em in the sea at the first opportunity!'

Shut-your-trap! heard them and decided to join in. 'Parrrabas is mad! Mad as a hatterrr!' he screeched.

Chapter II

Heehee, the Indian

By early evening the next day, more boats had joined them on the ocean. The coast of New Spain was now visible on the horizon and the town of Campeche looked like a huge white shell.

'Do you think father's ship, the Marie-Louise, will be in port?' Louise asked as she stood at the prow with Parabas and her brother.

'No. Cap'n Roc would never take the risk of anchoring his ship right under his enemy's nose. Pirates aren't welcome in New Spain. He'll have sought refuge along the coast somewhere, well away from the garrisons. He'll make his way back to Campeche disguised as a lumberjack or a planter or some such thing. Once we've found shelter for the ship, we'll go into town and try to track him down.

He'll be hanging around the port, listening out for news of the Mayan gold.'

'You said "we"', queried Louise. 'Does that mean you're not going ashore alone this time?'

'You and two other men will come with me,' he answered, gesturing to Louise.

'But what about me?' asked Benjamin.

'You'll stay on board where On-the-Fence can keep an eye on you. I only need one of you kids with me so that Cap'n Roc will accept my conditions. You will serve as my hostage. In fact...' Parabas looked them straight in the eye now to stress his point, 'the fate of each one of you is dependant on how the other one acts. So don't go getting any clever ideas and above all, don't try to escape!'

The Angry Flea gave Campeche a wide berth then sailed back south of the town towards the coast. Forests lining the shore were broken only in a few places by a handful of fishing villages. The pirates were on the lookout for an inlet that the ship could navigate. The shoreline consisted of a series of beaches and lagoons. Then finally…

'Trim the sails!' Parabas ordered. 'I can see a way in between those trees.'

The ship slowed down and entered a channel that formed a large pool. It was concealed from view by a line of dunes planted with coconut and date palms.

'Camouflage the ship,' the captain ordered his crew once it was at anchor. 'And stay on the alert. We'll be back here within two days.'

The small boat took the marquis, two pirates and Louise ashore and then returned to the Angry Flea. The ship was soon hidden from view under a mass of palm branches and resembled a small, slightly crazy-looking wood.

*   *   *

Parabas, One-Eyed Jack, Scarface and Louise struggled through the forest, thrashing their swords at low branches and foliage that blocked their path. The only sounds to be heard were the cracking of branches underfoot, the swishing of sword blades and heavy breathing. From time to time, a bird would fly up from the undergrowth and cry out a warning signal.

'Don't stop,' ordered Parabas, nudging Louise in the back. 'They won't attack us.'

A little further on the trees thinned out, opening into a clearing full of freshly cut logs and tree stumps. Suddenly, they realised that they were being watched.

'There's someone over there,' Scarface remarked.

'A lumberjack, I suppose,' added One-Eyed Jack.

'Are you blind?' retorted his companion. 'He's carrying a rifle, not a hatchet.'

'He's not hostile,' the marquis reassured them. 'He's watching us rather than running away.'

'Perhaps he's not alone,' suggested Louise.

In her heart, she was wishing that their own adventure could have a fresh start, that this twist of fate would make trouble for the pirates and set her free again.

Sitting on a tree trunk, the man watched them approach. He seemed amused to see them on their guard, swishing their swords left and right, and couldn't suppress a small laugh as if he found them ridiculous.

'Hee, hee! Don't be afraid,' he said in Spanish as they reached him. 'The jungle hasn't eaten any strangers for a very long time. You're pirates aren't you? Only pirates would approach Campeche through the forest. Hee, hee! You pirates scour all the seas, but you're very careful to avoid the ports!'

'You seem like a clever man to me,' Parabas replied. 'I'm sure you keep an eye on who comes and goes around here. Other French men perhaps?'

'I didn't know Parabas spoke Spanish so well!' muttered Louise, astonished.

'He's a marquis,' Scarface reminded her. 'He's educated!'

The Indian turned a deaf ear to the marquis' question. Parabas suddenly tore the rifle from his hands.

'This rifle is French. That's a fleur de lys engraved on the cartridge belt.'

'The sea washed it ashore,' claimed the Indian.

Parabas grabbed the man by the hair and pulled him forward until they were almost eye to eye.

'You're lying! The salt water would have marked the leather. You've come across some French men and killed and robbed them.'

'No, no!'

'So? Did they give it to you in exchange for services rendered? You'd better tell me the truth if you want to save your skin.'

The man lowered his eyes as Parabas let go of him. When he looked up again, he glanced at Louise with a fleeting look of recognition that didn't escape the marquis.

'What's going on? Have you seen her before?'

'It's those eyes. I've seen those eyes before!'

'That settles it, he's seen Cap'n Roc,' Parabas told his companions.

'Does he know where he is?' cried Louise.

The man suddenly felt the cold point of a sword at his throat.

'What's your name?'

'Taneecoloojaspucali – it's a bit long. Hee, hee!'

'In that case, we'll just call you Heehee. Sit down, Heehee, and tell us what you've seen.'

In simple Spanish, Heehee revealed that a pirate returning from Campeche three days ago had given him the rifle and cartridge belt in return for his giving false directions to any other buccaneers or adventurers he came across.

'He took my brother with him as a guide,' Heehee explained.

'Cap'n Roc's cunning,' chuckled Scarface once Parabas had translated this. 'He knows that the lure of gold would attract any number of rogues and vagabonds. He wants the Mayan treasure for himself.'

Parabas took Louise by the shoulder and stood her in front of Heehee.

'This is the daughter of the man who gave you the rifle!' he declared.

The man stared at her intently. She had the strangest sensation that he was looking right into her soul.

'Yes,' he agreed. 'The eyes don't lie.'

'She wants to find her father. So don't lie to us. Where has he gone?'

'To Kukulkan's city,' Heehee announced.

'Kukulkan?'

'It's the name of the Plumed Serpent!'

'And where is this city?'

'Palenque, in the forest of the Snake River.'

'Cap'n Roc has had an excellent idea!' Parabas exclaimed. 'He got his information in Campeche, and now he's going to surprise the Spaniards by taking their gold at source, before they have the chance to load it onto their ships. In fact, once at sea, these ships will be so heavily protected by a mighty fleet that it would be impossible to board them. Whereas by mounting an ambush deep in the jungle… voila! Let's follow his tracks. And you – you're coming with us!' barked Parabas, turning to Heehee. 'You'll be our guide. I'll give you your rifle back once we've found Cap'n Roc. I'll even throw in my hat. On the other hand, if you try to cheat us…' he sliced his blade through the air to make the consequences quite clear. 'Come on, let's get back to the ship. That's what I call a mission accomplished!' he finished, putting his sword back in its scabbard.

On the way back, Louise and Heehee found themselves side by side, flanked by the two pirates.

'Do you understand my language a little?' Louise asked him.

'I French very bad,' he admitted. 'Hee, hee!'

'Is it true that I have the same eyes as my father?'

'Like ocean colour they are.'

'And what else is special about my father?'

'Fog in heart. Him have terrible enemy. He – no pity for they.'

'Fog?' Louise repeated.

'Sad. Alone. Him be betrayed.'

'Oi you, Heehee, shut your trap!' ordered Parabas.

'Hmmm, so you're worried?' Louise thought to herself. 'It was you, after all, who betrayed my father to the English. Lucky he managed to escape.' Then mimicking the parrot, she said out loud:

'He's afrrraid, Parrrabas! He's shiverrring under his big hat!'

Chapter III

Snake River

The next day, the Angry Flea – or El Cacahuete – sailed alongside an island from which numerous smoke columns arose.

'That's the island of Tris,' Heehee told them. 'It's a hiding place for buccaneers!'

'Load the cannons!' Parabas ordered his crew. 'And keep your eyes peeled. These buccaneers are as dangerous as a bunch of crocodiles!'

'Crrrocodiles!' screeched Shut-your-trap! 'Take shelterrr! It's about to kick off, son of a sharrrk!'

Two big canoes full of armed men suddenly shot out from a mass of vegetation and began paddling vigorously towards the Angry Flea.

'They're going to seize the ship,' Benjamin mumbled, his mouth dry.

'No!' Parabas corrected him. 'It's our supplies and medicines that interest them. They'll just be living on meat – probably tortoise smoked over wood!'

'We're not going to give them our supplies, are we?' said Louise indignantly.

'Certainly not! Give the order to fire,' the marquis ordered his second in command.

On-the-Fence gave the order and the bosun, who was in charge of manoeuvres, followed it through. Shutters were flung open along the hull and cannon mouths were thrust out of the gunports. Louise shivered with excitement at the thought of a fight.

'You two, take shelter in the cabin,' Parabas shouted, signalling to One-Eyed Jack to lead them to safety.

'No!' bellowed Louise.

Her protests were lost in a thunderous roar. The cannons had fired a broadside. Waterspouts shot up in front of the canoes, rocking them dangerously. The buccaneers yelled out, but the cannon fire had not deterred them. Shouting wildly, they hurled themselves onwards into the attack. Shots rang out. The cannons, now reloaded, were firing again. One of the canoes was smashed to pieces, throwing its occupants into the air along with a hail of debris. The second canoe drew back. But, far from giving up, the buccaneers paddled on towards the prow of the ship.

'They're trying to get out of range,' said On-the-Fence. 'They've got grappling hooks to board us. All hands on deck!' he bawled to round up the crew.

'I haven't got time to waste,' grumbled Parabas. 'We'll stand and fight another day. Helmsman, turn the ship on them.'

The Angry Flea veered slightly to one side. The buccaneers went mad when they saw the bowsprit turn to face them. Some of them fired on the hull, but it was like trying to stop a great monster with a few spears. At the last moment, they dropped their weapons and hurled themselves into the sea. Struck dead centre, the canoe was flung into the air and broke in two. The Angry Flea sailed on...

A little later, the sea took on a yellowish tinge as they approached a wide waterway that split the forest in two.

'It's the Rio Usumacinta – Snake River!' Heehee told them, pointing at the immense water course pouring out into the gulf. The ship slowed as the men folded back the lower sails, keeping only the topsail hoisted. They entered the mouth of the river.

'Deep it is,' Heehee confirmed to a sailor who was stretched out on the bowsprit, swinging the lead to take depth soundings. 'Rocks no. Sandbanks no. Crocodiles – many! Hee, hee!'

'Rrrououou!' whimpered Shut-your-trap!, hiding his head under his wing.

The river was bordered by jungle. Flower-covered creepers hung down like huge snakes. The trees were so densely packed that it was pitch black in the undergrowth.

'How do we know there aren't Mayan warriors hiding in those ferns, ready to fire arrows at us?' Benjamin wondered aloud.

'Parabas is sure that father came this way. So we should be able to get through, too,' Louise reassured him. 'Just think – he's only three days ahead of us...'

'On-the-Fence didn't have a map of this area to show me,' her brother went on, 'but he explained that time and distance are very deceptive in the jungle. You can wander round for days, travelling long distances, and still end up back where you started.'

'That just means that father might be even closer,' said Louise in an excited voice.

'Or, on the other hand, it could take forever to find him,' Benjamin responded gloomily.

'Oh, do stop being so pessimistic,' Louise sighed. 'Look around you – we're in the jungle! We dreamt about things like this when we were little. Don't you remember, it meant adventure to us: wild animals, Indians, cities of gold. We used to pretend we were conquistadors!'

'I just see everything as it really is,' Benjamin replied, justifying himself. 'We are pirates' prisoners. Black Beard and Red Mary are almost certainly on our tracks, and Parabas is only trying to find father so he can rob him,' he continued.

'Well, he hasn't found him yet!'

'Oh, wake up, Louise! With us as hostages, it's as if Parabas has already got him by the throat. Nobody's coming to help us.'

Louise shrugged her shoulders. She didn't want to think about the dangers they faced. Once they found their father, it would all be alright. For the moment her head was full of dreams and she was sure that all would turn out well.

The ship slowly followed the course of the river. Not a soul was to be seen on the banks. Not even a single fisherman or hunter. And yet the pirates were totally convinced they were being watched. When the evening shadows cast darkness over the river, Parabas ordered the crew to drop anchor

in the middle and posted armed lookouts on the masts.

Night fell. The damp, humid air of the jungle was heavy with the sounds of jaguars growling, the strident cries of monkeys and the creaking of trees. A night filled with the sounds of hunters and hunted: sudden noises, cries of pain and then silence.

At dawn came a grinding sound as the crew weighed anchor. The sails filled and the ship continued its voyage along Snake River.

'Do we have far to go?' asked Parabas impatiently, peering at the river banks through his telescope.

Heehee made a sign to indicate that they still had a long way to go – a long way into an unknown world. Towards midday, he signalled that they had almost arrived, and Parabas sighted something unexpected through his telescope.

'The devil take us!' he cried. There was a ship lying on her side against the bank. Her masts were broken and her ropes and sails were all of a tangle.

There was a huge hole in her hull as though a giant had trodden on it. Crocodiles basked on her hull whilst others thrashed around inside the ship, striking their tails on the water with a whip-cracking sound.

'The wood hasn't rotted,' On-the-Fence observed as the Angry Flea approached the wreck. 'That means that it didn't happen very long ago.'

Suddenly Louise's voice rang out. 'Look at the name. It's the Marie-Louise. It's father's ship!'

Chapter IV

The cry of the quetzal

Orders flew back and forth on the Angry Flea. Parabas and some of the pirates launched the rowing boat into the water. It took only a few oar strokes to reach the Marie-Louise. They fired shots to disperse the crocodiles. At first, the creatures were reluctant to move. They stood their ground and snapped their jaws, but eventually slithered into the river and disappeared. Swords and pistols at the ready, Parabas and his men entered the ship through the hole in her hull. There was about a metre of water inside. Barrels and sacks had split open and were floating on the surface.

'I can't see any bodies,' said One-Eyed Jack.

'Maybe the crocodiles ate them,' suggested the bosun.

'Cannon fire couldn't have done this kind of damage,' Parabas reflected, examining the huge hole. 'I think an axe has been taken to the ship!'

They went outside and walked around her hull.

'I think I can guess what's happened,' he announced. 'Cap'n Roc must have gone into the jungle with most of his men, leaving his ship under the watch of a skeleton crew. That's when the Marie-Louise would have been attacked and destroyed. But the question is who did it? Natives? A band of robbers? Or Spanish soldiers?'

The question was met by a resounding silence as everyone looked around, anticipating the swishing sound of an arrow or the crack of a bullet at any moment. Scarface was examining the decks and sections of the mast. All of a sudden, he struck at the water with his weapon, let out a curse and rushed to join his companions on dry land.

'Those 'orrible crocodiles are back!' he exclaimed. 'I found some bullets in the wood, but not many. What's for certain is that it wasn't Indians who attacked the Marie-Louise.'

'Let's go back and calm those two brats down,' said Parabas. 'I don't want them jumping into the river and being eaten by crocodiles because they're desperate to find out what's happening.'

Leaning over the rail, Benjamin and Louise were firing questions at them as the small boat came alongside the Angry Flea.

'Cap'n Roc is alive,' Parabas reassured them.

'How do you know?' snapped Louise.

Parabas waited until he was back on board, then explained: 'No-one could have reduced a ship like the Marie-Louise to this state if a full crew had been on board. If they'd tried, we would have found much more evidence of a fight – broken blades, bullet holes everywhere and traces of blood. Those men left on the Marie-Louise must have been caught by surprise. They've probably been taken prisoner, and the ship has been disabled in order to prevent her breaking loose into the river and attracting attention.'

'So father is trapped in the jungle,' Benjamin concluded.

'And his enemies are hot on his heels!' Louise added. 'What are we waiting for? Let's go and rescue him!'

'Rrrescue him!' repeated Shut-your-trap! 'Billy goat's horrrn, shiverrr me timberrrs!'

'And you're coming with us!' said Louise decisively to Parabas.

'I presumed that's what you meant!' Parabas retorted. 'Now that I'm so near my prize, I need you two so that I can negotiate with your father. A daughter for the treasure map, a son for the Plumed Serpent's gold. I don't like the idea of the ship staying at anchor here,' he added, talking to On-the-Fence. 'The best thing is for you to head back to the open sea. We'll hide the small boat in the undergrowth and rendezvous with you on the coast in four days time. If you don't see us by then, mount an expedition to find us!'

A few minutes later, Parabas, a handful of men and both children watched as the ship departed, whilst Heehee hid the small boat beneath a screen of high ferns.

'I'll make the cry of the quetzal as we go along,' the Indian told Parabas as they started off into the thick jungle.

'Why's that?' the marquis asked. 'Do you want to give us away?'

'The quetzal is a very timid bird. If people are around, it keeps quiet. If not, it will reply with the same cry.'

Heehee glanced over his shoulder and made a

sound like a turtledove singing. The pirates listened to Parabas' explanation of what Heehee was doing. They pulled faces in disbelief that one bird cry could be picked up over the racket that the monkeys and birds were making. Heehee's face broke into a broad

smile. He raised his finger to indicate that they should all listen, then gestured to them to carry on walking.

'He's just making a fool of us, isn't he?' muttered

Louise. 'Surely he doesn't think we believe that quetzals will be our lookouts from here to the city?'

'Native Indians hear and see things that we don't notice,' Benjamin explained.

'Hmm. I think he's just trying to make himself seem useful to justify more of a reward. Parabas doesn't look as if he believes him any more than I do!'

The pirates moved onwards in single file, each following the exact footprints of the man ahead. The ground underfoot was treacherous: waterlogged moss that was riddled with potholes and roots. Giant lilies floated on top of deep pools of water. Rotting tree trunks that lay across the path created obstacles to get round or clamber over. With vines hanging down everywhere it was difficult to distinguish between plants and snakes. Heehee made his bird call again. Shut-your-trap! imitated him by calling out 'Rrrououou.' And he was the one that got an answer – from a family of parrots.

Flower heads flew as the pirates carved a path with their swords, frequently waving them overhead to fend off clouds of mosquitoes. Nearby, a fallen tree groaned and eyes suddenly emerged from a pond. What had looked like a large tree-trunk began to move, opening a mouth as big as an oven. They all ran for their lives to escape the crocodile's gnashing teeth. The air was damp and their shirts were soaked with sweat. Their legs felt heavy, making it difficult to walk – so much so that Parabas increased the rest periods.

When Heehee at last suggested stopping for the night, they threw themselves down on the ground, exhausted. One-Eyed Jack had landed on an ants' nest and he promptly leapt up again, scratching himself furiously.

'Do you think father is still in the Plumed Serpent's city?' asked Louise, chewing on a piece of dried meat as Parabas hadn't let them light a fire.

'Well, we haven't seen him heading back to the river. According to Heehee, the track we're taking is the easiest one to follow. If he's weighed down with gold, Cap'n Roc will surely choose this way, too.'

'I can't stop thinking about who destroyed the

Marie-Louise,' Benjamin went on. 'They must be somewhere between us and father, for sure.'

'I've had a long talk with our guide, Heehee,' Parabas told them. 'He's convinced that it was a band of robbers that attacked the ship, taking advantage of its poor defence. According to him, they wouldn't tangle with your father. Whatever they found on the ship would satisfy them well enough.'

'If not, we'll surprise them from behind in any case. Trapped between Cap'n Roc and us, they'll soon surrender.'

'So you are father's only remaining enemy!' Benjamin declared. 'If he gave you the Plumed Serpent's gold, would that not satisfy you?'

'I've been after his treasure map for so long that I'd feel I'd let myself down if I made do with the Mayan treasure,' replied Parabas.

'You scoundrel!' muttered Louise, giving him a scornful look. 'You want to steal everything he has!'

'Thanks to me, you'll find your father, and he'll find his dear children. Isn't that a kind of treasure, too?'

Just at that moment, Heehee made the cry of the quetzal up towards the tree-tops. Almost immediately, an identical cry came back to him. It could be heard quite clearly despite the noisy cackling of a flock of budgerigars.

'City near is,' the Indian announced in broken French so that everyone could understand. 'Quetzals many are in Palenque. The gods stick them's feathers in skin of snake. So Kukulkan is great feather serpent. Hee hee!'

'Charming,' muttered Louise.

'We need some sleep now,' Parabas advised them as he got up to organise the watch. 'Tomorrow will mark the end of your adventures!'

Chapter V

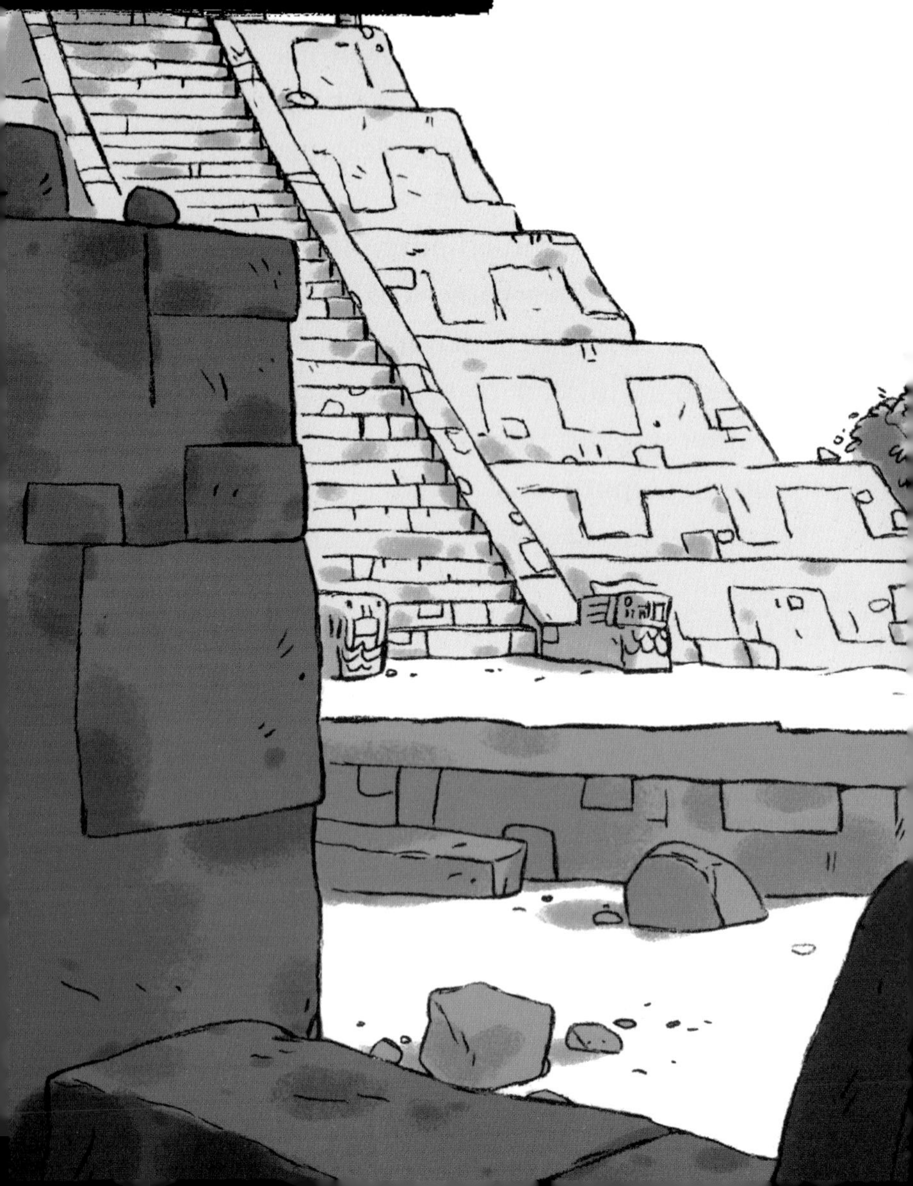

The city of the Plumed Serpent

At dawn, pools of water that had collected in the folds of large leaves dripped down from one level of vegetation to the next. A mist hung over the trees, giving them a ghostly appearance.

'Is it raining?' Benjamin asked. The water dripping onto his forehead had woken him up.

Heehee crouched down and explained to him that the jungle was alive. 'Trees, they breathing. Breath of Kukulkan. Milk of the gods,' he finished, opening his mouth to catch the water dripping down.

'Get up!' ordered Parabas, waking the pirates with a kick. 'Fortune awaits us. You can eat and drink as you walk.'

They set off in single file once again. The

children's hearts were thumping. Their father was so close. They felt as if the jungle was suddenly about to open up, like a page turning in a book, to bring them face to face with him.

'I'm scared,' sighed Louise. 'Scared that father will leave us with Parabas. What if he chooses to keep his treasure rather than free us?'

Benjamin said nothing. It was just the sort of question he'd been turning over in his head all night long. He, too, was really worried about meeting up with their father. It could just end in a huge fight...

Up front, Heehee suddenly gave the signal to stop. He made his bird call and back came the response as clear as the cry he had sent.

'We're here!' Parabas announced.

A shiver of excitement ran through the ranks. The men loaded their rifles and pistols and took hold of their swords and sabres. Benjamin and Louise exchanged glances. You could feel the tension. Everyone held their breath. Suddenly, Parabas gestured and gave the order to advance.

Golden rays of sunlight peeped through the treetops. Heehee pulled back the palms and a cascade of light flooded in.

'The city of Kukulkan!' he confirmed, pointing at it with his outstretched arm. The pirates emerged from the jungle. An abandoned city, partly covered with vegetation, spread out before them. Massive stone staircases climbed to the temples that stood on top of terraced pyramids. A different looking building, flanked by a square tower, occupied a large area in front of the highest pyramid.

'The palace of the ancient kings,' Heehee told them, pausing in front of it.

They spilled out into the small square. A deadly silence filled the city, as if the Plumed Serpent was sleeping amongst these ancient stones.

'Is there any gold in these ruins?' asked One-Eyed Jack, getting straight to the point.

'Treasure in temple is there,' answered Heehee in French.

'Where's father?' asked Louise. 'There's no-one here apart from us.'

'Cap'n Roc must have left by a different route,' groaned Parabas, clearly frustrated.

'Let's see if he's left any gold behind!' suggested One-Eyed Jack. He was getting excited.

'It's more important to catch Cap'n Roc,' Parabas reminded him. 'His treasure is way beyond anything you'll find here.'

But the very fact that they might actually get their hands on some real gold excited the pirates so much that they were no longer listening to their captain. They ran towards the big temple and started climbing the steps leading up to it.

'Bunch of idiots!' fumed Parabas.

'Idiots! Crrretins! Numbskulls!' added Shut-your-trap! for good measure.

'Okay, why don't we all go and have a look?' grumbled the marquis to Heehee and the two children.

'Give me back my rifle!' the Indian demanded. 'And give me the hat you promised me.'

Parabas handed over the weapon. 'You'll get the hat when we've got Cap'n Roc.'

He started climbing the pyramid. Just then Louise noticed Heehee giving a signal.

'What the…?' She didn't get to finish her sentence. The Indian had just aimed the rifle at Parabas and opened fire, hitting him in the thigh. Parabas collapsed and fell down several steps. The children were shocked. Was Heehee trying to help them or… The pirates stopped and looked back at them. Then Heehee lifted his arms skywards, turned towards the palace and gave a loud whoop of victory.

'Filthy traitor!' croaked Parabas, pointing his pistol towards the Indian. He fired, and Heehee fell down, stone dead. At that moment, Spanish soldiers surged from the building, yelling at the tops of their voices.

'We… we've fallen into an ambush,' Benjamin stammered.

'An ambush!' Shut-your-trap! was going wild. 'To arrrms! Load the cannons! It's all going crrrazy, son of a sharrrk!'

There was the sound of gunfire. Two pirates sank

to their knees. Louise grabbed Parabas' sword and scowled up at the soldiers. 'Come on! I'll cut you to pieces,' she cried, brandishing the blade.

But Benjamin grabbed her from behind and, pulling her down, he pinned her to the ground.

'Do you want to get us killed?' he hissed. 'We stand no chance against them.'

The soldiers rushed towards the pyramid. They shoved Parabas aside and began mounting the great staircase. Several hands grasped hold of the children and pulled them to their feet. Powerless, Benjamin and Louise could only watch the attack. The pirates were holed up in the temple, which consisted of only a single room. They discharged their weapons against the Spanish soldiers.

'We're trapped,' groaned One-Eyed Jack. 'And the cap'n's already been taken prisoner.'

'That Indian betrayed us,' said Scarface. 'There's no treasure in this temple, nor a gram of gold in this accursed city. This is what I think of the Plumed Serpent!'

In his fury, he seized a stone statue representing

the god Kukulkan that was mounted on a pedestal in the centre of the temple. He hurled it outside. The statue smashed on the steps and its head tumbled right to the bottom of the staircase. With that, a terrifying rumbling sound rose from the jungle, the ground began to tremble and the trees shook as if a powerful gale was hurtling through them. Everyone looked up from the fight, fearing an earthquake.

'Kukulkan is very angry!' shouted an Indian who was crouching beside Heehee. 'He will take revenge for the insult the white men did to him and for the death of Taneecoloojaspucali!'

Louise leaned towards Benjamin and whispered: 'He looks just like Heehee. I'm sure it's his brother, the one who guided father here.'

'Do you think he gave him up to the Spanish?' Benjamin asked. Louise was about to reply when a Spanish officer cut her off. 'You're French!' he exclaimed in their language. The children nodded their heads. The man gave a satisfied smile as the pirates threw down their weapons and came out of the temple, their arms held high.

'The thought of gold makes them crazy with greed,' he continued in French. 'That's the second French lot we've captured in three days. I suppose the English and Dutch pirates will soon show up here too!'

'Have you got Cap'n Roc?' asked Louise.

'Yes. His Indian guide led him right into our net!'

'How did you know we'd head for Palenque?' asked Parabas, between groans of pain.

'Well, it's the lure of gold, isn't it?' said the officer. 'The very word makes everyone throw caution to the wind!'

As his soldiers brought the pirates down from the pyramid, he briefly explained.

'I'll tell you this because you won't dare to repeat it. In actual fact, there was no treasure in this city. The real gold will be loaded onto our galleons in Carthagena in Columbia. The solid gold statues and Inca jewellery have been smelted down into ingots. They are on their way from Peru to the port. We wanted to keep our galleons safe when they were transporting the gold to Spain, so the viceroy had the idea of laying a trap. A rumour was spread that would direct the pirates somewhere completely different. We're expecting plenty more scoundrels to show up, but we were delighted to get our hands on Cap'n Roc. He's one of the most famous pirates in the Caribbean!'

'Where is he?' pleaded Louise. She was so angry

that she was on the verge of tears. 'What are you going to do with him?'

'What we do with all pirates when we catch them – take 'em on a forced march to Veracruz, where they are tried and hanged. You two will escape the hangman's rope because you're too young, but you won't avoid prison!'

The officer went over to his men to give them orders. The prisoners were bound or shackled while the wounded were given some basic first aid.

'The cry of the quetzal, that was to let you know we were coming, I suppose,' said Benjamin, watching a man bandaging Parabas' thigh. 'The "bird" that replied must have been Heehee's brother.'

'That Indian made a fool of us all from the start,' Parabas remarked bitterly. 'He let Cap'n Roc believe he'd stop other pirates taking the same path as him, but he waited for his prey in the clearing to lead them into the Spanish ambush. Who knows how many other Brothers of the Coast he'd have led into the same trap?'

'So do you think the Spanish destroyed the Marie-Louise to cut off father's retreat?' asked Benjamin.

'Without a doubt,' Parabas replied. 'I did well to send the Angry Flea back to sea.'

'I wish we could go aboard her now,' sighed Louise, clenching her fists.

Then their hands were chained behind their backs. The officer designated ten soldiers and several native porters to escort the pirates to Veracruz. Then he ordered the rest of his men to remove all traces of the skirmish and to conceal themselves in the palace once again. His Indian scouts had warned him that the cry of the quetzal had been heard again from the direction of Snake River.

Chapter VI

The wrath of
the Great Jungle

The children trudged along, dragging their feet. The soldiers prodded the pirates with their swords to make them go faster. The weakest ones were supported by their crewmates. Shut-your-trap! was perched on the marquis' shoulder, half hidden by his big hat.

'Parabas didn't know how right he was last night when he said today would be the end of our adventures,' Louise grumbled. 'We'll only see father when his body is hanging at the end of a rope.'

'And what about us?' groaned Benjamin. 'What will become of us?'

The jungle around them was full of sounds. Birds trilled, monkeys chattered, trees creaked and grasses whistled. Suddenly there was silence. A heavy silence, as if some monstrous presence had just descended on the place. The porters glanced around them. They seemed nervous and exchanged words in their own dialect. The sergeant in charge of the expedition gave orders, hoping he sounded confident enough to quell the fear that seemed to be spreading amongst them. He doubled the speed of the march, ignoring the protests of the wounded.

'What does it matter if they arrive dead or alive,' he told his men. 'When all's said and done, it's death that awaits them.'

'I don't understand what he's saying, but I'm sure he's worried,' whispered Benjamin. 'I think someone or something is hiding in the undergrowth, watching us.'

'I feel it, too,' Louise agreed. 'Perhaps it's a jaguar.'

'Kukulkan, Kukulkan,' the natives began to chant, cowering as if they were afraid that the trees would lash out at them.

The sergeant ordered them to be quiet and to walk faster. He threatened to beat them if they spread fear amongst the others. They passed under a large clump of intertwined creepers and were struggling through a maze of bushes when a terrible cry froze them in their tracks. The children clung to one another. Some of the soldiers fired their rifles and one of the porters dropped his load and ran off. The sergeant turned his gun on the others to stop them doing likewise.

'What's… what's happening?' stammered Louise. Benjamin had no answer.

'Kukulkan, Kukulkan,' chanted the Indians. Their voices were getting more and more frenzied.

'They must believe that the Plumed Serpent is taking revenge for the broken statue,' Benjamin guessed, finally making sense of it.

'That cry – it was horrible!' Louise shuddered. 'It was half human and half animal. We're not going to get out of this jungle alive, are we?' she whispered. 'It's not a jungle – it's something terrifying… it's going to swallow us up!'

The soldiers kept their eyes fixed on the undergrowth around them, ready to fire at the slightest movement. Suddenly, one of them clutched his hand to his head and collapsed. The astonished sergeant bent down and turned him over to examine him. He discovered a deep wound in the soldier's forehead, but there was no sign of what had caused it.

'He didn't even walk into a branch,' he said, perplexed.

Suddenly, one of the pirates dropped down as if someone had cut off his legs. Now there was panic! The porters dropped their bundles and ran. The air was filled with a whistling sound as arrows and stones rained down on them. The leaves around them parted.

'Look out!' Louise screamed.

Mayan warriors sprang out like demons. They wore headdresses made from snakeheads which were decorated with scales and feathers. They brandished bows, slings, clubs and great wooden sticks tipped with sharp flintheads.

'Stay together,' shouted the sergeant. 'Form a square and defend yourselves!'

But no-one obeyed him. Almost everyone fled to save their own skin. The warriors raced after them, striking out at soldiers and prisoners alike. Shots rang out, but it didn't slow the Mayans down. Cries of terror were mingled with fierce war cries in the ensuing chase. It was pointless to try to escape, so Benjamin and Louise hid under a canopy of leaves at the foot of a banana tree. The manacles that bound their wrists were big enough for an adult. The children struggled frantically to wrench their hands free of them. They succeeded!

'They must be snake-men,' Louise shivered. 'The warriors of Kukulkan. You were right about the porter's fear – the warriors want to avenge the insult to their god. They must have had lookouts hiding in the ruins of the city.'

'Oh no, one of them is coming back this way!'

They held their breath, wishing that the earth would swallow them up. The warrior beat the bushes with his stick, trying to root out any remaining enemies. His head seemed to poke out from the gaping jaws of a boa constrictor and its skin trailed down to his ankles. The snakeskin was worn like a cloak and was covered with different coloured feathers. The children's hearts were pounding so loudly and it seemed impossible that the warrior wouldn't hear them. 'We're not going to sit here and be plucked like fledglings from a nest,' Louise thought to herself. She got ready to spring out of her hiding place, but the snake-man suddenly turned on his heels and, yelling wildly, rushed towards a thicket. As he lunged at a soldier who was trying to pass unnoticed, the children took advantage of the distraction to clamber through the leaves and slide down a slope.

'Run!' Benjamin hissed.

Shots rang out behind them. That was it, they'd been spotted. No time to lose! They were scratched and whipped by low branches and palm fronds as they fled. Sometimes their path was blocked by roots that looked just like snakes in the long grass. They stumbled, tripped and scrambled up again to run on with a manic desperation. They heard a rustling to their right. Instinctively they veered left to follow an animal's well-trodden path through the undergrowth, and came face to face with a family of wild pigs. They screamed and the pigs ran off. Then a great weight fell on their shoulders and pinned them to the ground. 'We must be dead...' was all Benjamin could think.

Chapter VII

The devil's gift

Hands were clamped over the children's mouths. The weight pinning them to the ground prevented them from moving.

'What's going on?' Louise wondered, as each minute passed and nothing happened. 'Why don't they kill us?'

She heard footsteps approaching and words being spoken in an unknown language. Suddenly, there was the flurried sound of a hunt, punctuated by grunting and squealing. The snakemen's laughter came from further off now.

'You'd better thank those little pigs,' a voice murmured in Louise's ear. 'They've just saved our lives.'

Louise shuddered. That voice. It was impossible.

It couldn't be... She lifted her head slightly and saw Malibu lying on top of her brother and Tepos crouched by a huge fern, arrow primed and ready to defend them. The weight was Red Mary – who was sitting on top of her! But how had she found them?

The sounds of combat had ended. Silence reigned in the jungle. One by one, the timid tweeting of the birds began again. Once the trees had filled with noise, the monkeys broke their silence and went back to their usual noisy acrobatics.

'That's it,' declared Mary, allowing Louise to sit up.

'Kukulkan is calm. The soldiers and their prisoners must have died in the jungle. A sad end for Parabas, but being hanged is no better a fate.'

'I suppose you're after the Plumed Serpent's gold, too,' said Benjamin to his half-sister. 'All the pirates of the Caribbean are going to fall into this trap.'

'There's no gold in the city,' Louise explained.

'The Spanish set up a rumour to fool the pirates. Father's been taken captive. The soldiers have taken him to Veracruz and he's going to be hanged there. It was his guide who betrayed him.'

'Our guide gave us up to the Spanish, too,' added Benjamin.

'That's why I only trust my Uncle Tepos,' their half-sister said. 'He knows the jungle well, and that's why we came via the Great Jungle rather than the river – luckily for you two!' she finished with a cunning smile.

'We have to save father!' cried Louise. 'Let's

attack Veracruz and smash our way into the prison!
You've got a ship with cannons and a crew, haven't
you?' she persisted, since Mary hadn't replied. 'We
can even get the Angry Flea to help us. On-the-
Fence will...'

Mary interrupted her. 'Let's go back to my ship,
the Capricious. We've nothing more to do here.'

Just as they set out, a whirlwind of feathers
descended on them.

'Shut-your-trap!, it's you!' cried Benjamin. 'So
you managed to dodge all the arrows.'

Quite out of character, the bird remained silent

and took refuge on the boy's shoulder. 'He must be really frightened to be so quiet,' Louise commented.

'What can we do for father?' she asked her half-sister.

'He abandoned us all when we were very young, myself and you two,' Red Mary growled. 'He'd deserve it if we didn't care what happened to him.'

Mary's words gave the children's hearts a tiny glimmer of hope.

'What do you mean by that?' Louise asked.

'Well, we wouldn't want his half of the map to be lost forever, would we?'

'The trrreasure map!' squawked Shut-your-trap! excitedly. 'Gold! Gold everrrywherrre!'

'This bird's recovered quickly,' laughed Benjamin.

He waited until they'd passed through a difficult part of the track, then asked Mary: 'Why did you save Louise and me? The warriors of the Plumed Serpent would have finished us off. Is it because you care about us…?'

Tepos put a hand on his shoulder. 'That's enough questions for one day. You'll get all your answers in good time.'

Back where the attack had taken place, a soldier's body moved. It began rocking back and forth, then it rolled over to one side to reveal Parabas underneath. The marquis pulled himself up. He managed to unsheathe the sword that hung from the Spanish soldier's belt and, wedging it between his feet, he set about cutting the leather thong which bound his wrists. Just then, there was a rustling sound close by and someone's back slowly arched up. It was One-Eyed Jack, emerging from amongst the bodies. Further over, two legs were trying to kick free of a soldier's body that had fallen on top of them. It was Scarface's legs!

'We're not in great shape, old mates,' said Parabas, dragging himself towards them, 'but we'll live to fight another day, and that's what matters!'

'I think we're the only ones who escaped,' said One-Eyed Jack. 'Now I know that my skull is tougher than a club.'

'I've been hit in the shoulder by an arrow,' Scarface groaned, 'but I've still got one good arm.'

'As for me, I had the good fortune to be knocked to the ground by the sergeant when he was hit. I lay beneath him and played dead. I was already covered in blood, so I fooled the warriors. The devil didn't want to take us this time!' Parabas concluded. 'He protects his own creatures. He'll give us the strength to get back to the Angry Flea.'

'And then?' asked One-Eyed Jack, helping Scarface to his feet.

'Then? Then we'll go looking for Cap'n Roc's treasure!'

'The brats have disappeared,' One-Eyed Jack warned him. 'Either they're lost in the jungle or the Mayans have carried them off.'

'I don't need them any more to get to their father. Where he is now, he can't escape me!'

His laughter rang out high into the trees, cutting through the babbling sounds of the jungle. A parrot cried out, trying to imitate him. 'You're wasting your time,' Parabas mocked him. 'You need to be a pirate to have the devil's laugh!'

ABOUT THE AUTHOR

Alain Surget is a professor of history as well as a prolific novelist. He started writing plays and poetry at the early age of 14, then went on to write over 50 novels. Many of these are set in Ancient Egypt, or have animal conservation as their theme.

Alain is married with three children and lives in Metz, France. Despite writing about the sea in the Jolly Roger series of novels, he rarely sets foot in it, preferring life in the mountains.

ABOUT THE ILLUSTRATOR

Annette Marnat loved drawing as a child, and went on to study illustration in Lyon, where she still lives. When she graduated in 2004, her work was selected for the Bologna Children's Book Fair Illustrators catalogue, and commissions from publishers soon followed. She is now a well-established and popular children's book illustrator.

PEOPLE AND PLACES

NEW SPAIN

An area in North America which was colonised by Spanish conquistador Hernan Cortés in the 16th Century, after the fall of the Aztec empire. Much of this region is today known as Mexico.

CAMPECHE

A state in the far east of Mexico which was once home to the ancient Mayan culture.

VERACRUZ

A coastal region in the east of Mexico used by Cortés as an entry point for the conquest of what would become New Spain.

MAYA CIVILISATION

Formed as early as 1500 BC, the Maya civilisation occupied the Yucatán peninsula of Mexico. They developed astronomy, calendar systems and writing, and built observatories to watch stars.

CONTENTS

OTHER TITLES IN THIS SERIES

1. THE PIRATE'S LEGACY

Orphaned by their mother's death, twins Louise and Benjamin find themselves living in a grim Parisian poorhouse. Soon they decide to escape and reclaim their freedom! Their journey takes them to St Malo, where they cross paths with Black Beard – a scary pirate who has some very shocking news for them...

2. THE GHOST SHIP

Setting sail on The Angry Flea in search of their father, Louise and Benjamin discover what a pirate's life is like. They soon find that it's not plain sailing! During a frightening storm, they are thrown aboard a ship manned by a crew of rotting skeletons... the legendary ghost ship The Flying Dutchman!

3. SHARK ISLAND

When the twins stumble across a secret hideout on 'Shark Island', they find themselves trapped. The two young pirates must find a way out quickly or risk losing their father's trail.